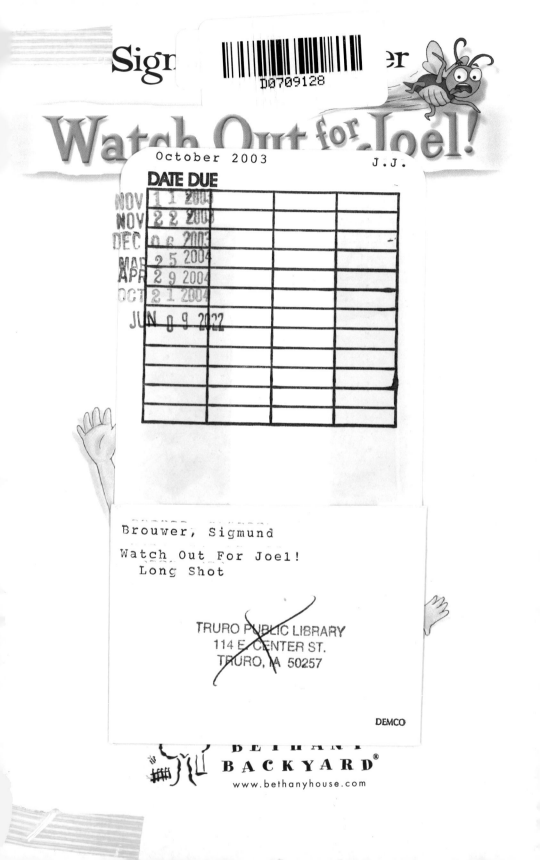

Sign_____er

D0709128

Watch Out for Joel!

October 2003   J.J.

DATE DUE

NOV 1 1 2003			
NOV 2 2 2003			
DEC 0 6 2003			
MAR 2 5 2004			
APR 2 9 2004			
OCT 2 1 2004			
JUN 0 9 2022			

Brouwer, Sigmund

Watch Out For Joel!
Long Shot

DEMCO

BETHANY
BACKYARD®
www.bethanyhouse.com

Published by Bethany House Publishers
11400 Hampshire Avenue South
Bloomington, Minnesota 55438
www.bethanyhouse.com

Bethany House Publishers is a Division of
Baker Book House Company, Grand Rapids, Michigan.

Printed in China

Library of Congress Cataloging-in-Publication Data

Brouwer, Sigmund, 1959–
   Long shot / by Sigmund Brouwer.
     p. cm. – (Watch out for Joel!)
Summary: Seven-year-old Joel watches disapprovingly while his brother and cousin
make the world's largest slingshot.
   ISBN 0-7642-2581-2
   [1. Honesty—Fiction.] I. Title.
   PZ7.B79984 Lm   2002
   [Fic]–dc21

                                             2002006131

Honesty Is the Best Policy

When Ricky and Lisa build the world's biggest slingshot, something very bad happens! Will they be able to hide their mistake?

Proverbs 12:22 says, "Lips that lie are disgusting to the Lord, but honest people are his delight." Ricky and Lisa need to learn to tell the truth. As you read the story, can you think of a time when you acted like Ricky and Lisa?

1

In the summer, Joel and his older brother, Ricky, went to a farm to visit their cousin Lisa.

It was a Saturday morning. Lisa's mother and father went into town for the day.

Joel and Lisa and Ricky stood outside near a barn and a fence.

"I have an idea," Lisa said. She pointed at a pond near the barn. "I want to build the biggest slingshot in the world. Then we could shoot a big rock into the water of the pond."

Joel pointed at the ducks in the pond. "What if you hit a duck?" Joel asked.

Lisa was thirteen years old. So was Ricky.

"What do you know?" Ricky asked Joel. "You are only seven years old."

"What do you know?" Lisa asked Joel. "If we use a big rock, they will see the shadow of the rock before it gets close. The shadow will scare the ducks. And the ducks will fly away before the rock can hit them. The rock will not hit the ducks."

"What do I know?" Joel said. "I am only seven."

So Ricky and his cousin Lisa started to build the biggest slingshot in the world.

2

First, Ricky and Lisa pounded two big fence posts into the ground. The big fence posts were ten feet apart.

Then Ricky and Lisa found six bicycle tire tubes. They cut them into long rubber strips.

Ricky and Lisa nailed the ends of three tire tubes near the top of one post. They nailed the ends of the other three tire tubes near the top of the other post.

Ricky and Lisa tied the loose ends of all the rubber strips to a big patch of leather.

They had made the biggest slingshot in the world.

"Are you sure this is a good idea?" Joel asked.

"What do you know?" Ricky and Lisa said. "You are only seven."

Lisa found a rock.

"Look," she said. "This is the right size."

She showed the rock to Joel and Ricky. The rock was the size of a baseball.

"You are right," Ricky said. "It is the right size."

"Are you sure this is a good idea?" Joel asked.

"What do you know?" Ricky and Lisa said. "You are only seven."

Ricky and Lisa put the rock in the leather patch.

Ricky and Lisa pulled the rubber bands tight. They held on to the rock and stepped back.

They stepped back some more.

"Are you sure this is a good idea?" Joel asked.

"What do you know?" Ricky and Lisa said. "You are only seven."

3

Ricky and Lisa stepped back even farther until the rubber was so tight they could not hold on anymore.

They let go. They shot the big rock at the pond. The rock went high into the air. Just like it had been shot from a cannon.

"Wow," Lisa said.

"Wow," Ricky said.

The rock went higher and higher.

"Are you sure this is a good idea?" Joel asked as they all watched the rock.

"What do you know?" Ricky and Lisa said. "You are only seven."

The rock went higher and farther. It went far over the pond.

The rock went straight toward the cows on the other side of the pond.

"Oh no," Ricky said as he watched the big, flying rock go toward the cows.

"Oh no," Lisa said as she watched the big, flying rock go toward the cows.

"What do I know?" Joel said as he watched the big, flying rock go toward the cows. "I am only seven."

4

"Move, all you cows!" Ricky shouted.

"Move, all you cows!" Lisa shouted.

The rock kept going right at the cows.

The cows did not move.

"Run away!" Ricky shouted.

"Run away!" Lisa shouted.

The cows did not move. The cows did not run. The cows just stood there and ate grass. That is what cows do all day.

"Move, all you cows!" Ricky shouted.

"Move, all you cows!" Lisa shouted.

The rock from the biggest slingshot in the

world started to drop from the sky. Right in the middle of all the cows.

"Run away!" Ricky shouted.

"Run away!" Lisa shouted.

Thump. The rock hit a cow in the head. Slowly, it fell over. All the other cows ran away.

That is when Ricky and Lisa saw that they had not hit a cow. No, they had hit a big, big bull named Old Black.

Old Black did not get up.

"This is not good," Ricky said.

"You are right," Lisa said.

"What do I know?" Joel said. "I am only seven."

5

"Ricky," Lisa said as she looked at the big black bull on the ground. "I think you just killed the bull."

"Me?" Ricky said. "The slingshot was your idea."

"You helped me build it. You helped me shoot a rock. The rock hit the bull in the head. I did not do this alone."

"What will we do?" Ricky asked Lisa.

"My mom and dad will be back in about an hour," Lisa said. "We have got to hide the bull from them. Later, we can think of something else."

Ricky frowned. "We cannot just grab that bull by the ears and drag him away."

"I have an idea," Lisa said. "We can use my dad's tractor to drag the bull away."

"Do you know how to drive the tractor?" Ricky asked.

"Yes," Lisa told him. "My dad showed me how to drive it."

"Is it all right with your dad if we drive the tractor when he is away?" Ricky asked Lisa.

"Do you want to tell him we killed his bull?" Lisa asked.

"No," Ricky said. "Let's get the keys to the tractor."

"Do you think that is a good idea?" Joel asked.

"What do you know?" Lisa said.

"Right," Joel said. "I am only seven."

6

Lisa drove the tractor to Old Black.

Joel and Ricky followed. They stood beside the big, big bull.

Old Black did not move.

Joel and Ricky and Lisa stared down at Old Black.

"This is a big bull," Joel said. "Are you sure—"

"What do you know?" Ricky and Lisa said. "You are only seven."

Lisa tied two long pieces of rope to the back of the tractor.

Ricky tied the other ends of the ropes

around the horns of the bull. Ricky pulled the ropes tight.

"Ready?" Ricky asked Lisa.

"Ready," Lisa said.

Joel did not say anything. He was only seven.

Lisa hopped on the tractor. She tried to drive it away.

Old Black was too big. The tractor could not pull the bull.

Lisa tried to drive the tractor away again.

This time, the knots on the rope pulled apart. The rope came off the horns of the bull.

Lisa stopped the tractor. She helped Ricky tie the rope to the bull's horns again. They tied the rope even tighter than before.

Suddenly, the bull opened his eyes.

7

Old Black stared at Ricky and Lisa.

Ricky and Lisa stared at Old Black.

"Oh no," Ricky and Lisa said.

Joel did not say anything. He started to run.

Old Black jumped to his feet.

Old Black was not happy.

Ricky and Lisa ran, too.

Ricky and Lisa ran far.

Old Black did not run far at all. Old Black was still tied to the tractor with those long pieces of rope. He was still tied to the tractor by his horns.

Old Black was mad. Old Black made a lot of noise. Old Black tried to pull the tractor backward.

Ricky and Lisa stopped running.

They watched Old Black as he tried to pull the tractor.

Joel walked over to Ricky and Lisa. "This is not good," Joel said.

"What do you know?" Lisa said. "The bull is not dead. I think this is very good."

"What do you know?" Ricky said to Joel. "You are only seven."

"I know there is a bull tied to a tractor," Joel said. "I know when Lisa's dad gets here, he will see the bull tied to the tractor."

"What do you know?" Lisa said. "We will untie the bull and move the tractor."

"What do you know?" Ricky said to Joel. "You are only seven."

"Who will untie Old Black?" Joel asked. "That is what I want to know."

8

When Lisa's dad came back from town, Joel and Ricky and Lisa were still watching Old Black.

Old Black was still tied to the tractor.

Old Black was still angry, too.

Lisa's dad walked across the field to Joel and Ricky and Lisa and Old Black and the tractor.

Lisa's dad was tall in his cowboy boots. When he reached Joel and Ricky and Lisa, he took his cowboy hat off. He scratched his head as he looked at Old Black tied to the tractor.

Lisa's dad turned around and looked at the

biggest slingshot in the world.

He looked again at Old Black tied to the tractor.

"Well," Lisa's dad said. "Would anyone like to tell me what happened?"

"Not me," Joel said. "I am only seven."

Ricky and Lisa told Lisa's dad what happened.

Behind all of them, Old Black kept pulling on the tractor.

Old Black was still mad.

Old Black still made a lot of noise.

9

Lisa's dad did not know if he should be mad. Or if he should laugh.

"I know you did not hit the bull on purpose," Lisa's dad said. "It was a mistake."

"Yes," Lisa said. "We are sorry."

"Yes," Ricky said. "We are very sorry."

"When you make a mistake, you should not try to hide it from your parents," Lisa's dad said. "We love you and will help you learn from your mistakes."

"Yes," Lisa said.

"Yes," Ricky said.

"Yes," Joel said, even though he was only seven.

"Now I need to get an ax," Lisa's dad said.

"Do not hurt Old Black!" Lisa said.

"Of course not," Lisa's dad said. "I need to chop the rope. But I will do it from the truck."

Lisa's dad laughed. "I do not want to be around on foot when Old Black gets loose!"

A Lesson About Honesty

In *Long Shot*, Ricky and Lisa make a mistake, and then make it worse by trying to cover it up so no one will find out.

We all make mistakes in life. The important thing is to tell the truth and ask forgiveness for our mistakes. When we do, God gives us a fresh start. When we are honest with our parents about our mistakes, they can help fix the problem, rather than make it worse like Lisa and Ricky did.

To Talk About

1. Why is telling the truth important?

2. What does forgiveness mean?

3. What can you do to show God's love to others?

> *"I know, my God, that you test people's hearts. You are happy when people do what is right."*
> 1 Chronicles 29:17

Award-winning author Sigmund Brouwer inspires kids to love reading. From WATCH OUT FOR JOEL! to the ACCIDENTAL DETECTIVES series (full of stories about Joel's older brother, Ricky), Sigmund writes books that kids want to read again and again. Not only does he write cool books, Sigmund also holds writing camps and classes for more than ten thousand children each year!

You can read more about Sigmund, his books, and the Young Writer's Institute on his Web site, *www.coolreading.com*.